Prince [illegible]d F[illegible] S[illegible]ies

Level 3

Contents

Published by
Kuldeep Jain
for
Pegasus
An imprint of
B. Jain Publishers (P) Ltd.
1921, Street No. 10, Chuna Mandi, Paharganj, New Delhi-110055 (INDIA)
Phones: 91-11-4567 1000 | Fax: 91-11-4567 1010
Website: **www.bjain.com** | E-mail: **info@bjain.com**

THUMBELINA

Let's know about Hans Christian Andersen

The Story *Thumbelina* was written by **Hans Christian Andersen** who was a Danish author, fairy tale writer, and poet, noted for his children's stories.

Hans Christian Andersen was born on April 2, 1805, in Odense, Denmark. His father was a poor shoemaker and his mother was a washerwoman. At the age of fourteen, Andersen went to Copenhagen, Denmark, to try his luck.

After trying really hard for a long time, Andersen passed his university exams in 1828. He celebrated the passing of his university exams by writing his first narrative. The story was a success. Andersen quickly released a collection of poems. Andersen began his fairy tale writing by retelling folk tales he had heard as a child. However, soon, he began to compose his own stories. Most of his stories are original. The first volumes written from 1835 to 1837 contained nineteen stories and were called *Fairy Tales Told for Children*.

Once, upon a time there lived a woman, whose only wish was to have a child.

'If only I had a child, my house would be full of joy,' she often thought. At last, she went to a fairy and told her about her wish.

The fairy said, 'Your wish will be granted. Just take this barley corn, plant it in a pot in your house and tend it carefully.'

ew Words | granted
tend

The woman was pleased to hear this. She took the barley corn from the fairy and planted it in a pot.

A few days later, a beautiful tulip bud sprang out from the barley corn plant. The woman was very happy and she kissed the bud. Immediately, at her touch the petals opened and the woman gasped! A little girl who was no bigger than a thumb was sitting inside the bud!

'I will call my tiny child, Thumbelina,' cried the woman filled with joy.

The cradle of little Thumbelina was made from half the shell of a walnut, and was quilted with a rose petal.

Later one night, while Thumbelina was fast asleep in her bed an ugly toad hopped in from the window.

New Words | quilted
cradle

When the toad looked at Thumbelina, she croaked, 'This beautiful maiden can be a lovely bride for my son!'

New Words | maiden

The next moment, the toad lifted the little cradle with Thumbelina still fast asleep in it and hopped out of the window.

Now, the toad lived with her ugly son at the foot of the garden, near a stream. When the son saw little Thumbelina, he croaked with delight and wanted to know who she was.

New Words | delight

'Keep quiet, otherwise you will wake her up,' scolded the mother toad.

Then, the mother toad gently lifted Thumbelina from her cradle and laid her on a large leaf of a water lily in the stream.

'We will make a room for her under the mud and place her little cradle there,' said the mother toad to her son. At once, the two toads hopped towards their home.

New Words | scolded

Meanwhile, Thumbelina woke up. 'How did I end up on a leaf?' she wondered. Then, she saw that the leaf, she was sitting on, was surrounded by water on all sides. She was frightened and began to weep loudly.

Hearing her cries, the mother toad popped her head out of the water and said, 'I have brought you here and you will be my son's bride.'

New Words | weep

Saying this, the mother toad once again disappeared under water. When Thumbelina heard this, she started crying even harder. While Thumbelina sat their crying, a few fishes too had heard what the mother toad had told her.

'She must not marry the ugly toad,' said the fishes amongst themselves, when they looked at the beautiful little Thumbelina.

New Words | disappeared

'We must help her get away from here,' said a fish. 'We cannot take her away but we can gnaw at the stem of the water lily.'

So, without wasting any time, they began to bite the green stem of the leaf on which Thumbelina was sitting. A few minutes later, away floated the leaf carrying the little girl sitting on it. Thumbelina was happy to be going away from the toads. She floated for days and nights until the leaf stopped near the shore beside a cornfield.

Tired and hungry, Thumbelina walked through the cornfield, till she found a large tree with a small door in its trunk. The house belonged to a field mouse. Thumbelina knocked on the door. A moment later, the field mouse opened the door. Seeing the miserable condition Thumbelina was in, she took pity on her.

New Words		
	gnaw	cornfield
	miserable	pity

'Little girl, come in and dine with me,' said the field mouse.

Soon, the field mouse took a liking for Thumbelina.

She said, 'You can stay here, if you agree to keep the house clean.'

Thumbelina agreed and so she started staying with the field mouse.

One day, the field mouse told Thumbelina, 'Our neighbour, the rich Mole is coming to visit us. Unfortunately, he is blind. But he likes to listen to stories. It would be your great fortune if he would like to have you for a wife.'

Thumbelina didn't wish to marry the Mole. However, when the mole came, she told him delightful stories. The Mole fell in love with Thumbelina's voice and decided to marry her. But he did not say so at the moment.

Before he left, he told the field mouse, 'Friend, I have dug a tunnel from my house to yours though I cannot see. Would you like to see the tunnel?'

'Of course, we will see it,' said the field mouse. 'Won't we, Thumbelina?'

New Words | Unfortunately
fortune
delightful

Poor Thumbelina agreed. Soon, they had stepped out of the field mouse' house. Then, the mole said, 'I must warn you about a dead bird lying in the tunnel. Do not be alarmed at the sight.'

As they were walking through the tunnel, soon, they saw a bird lying on the ground. It was a swallow. 'Poor bird,' said the field mouse.

But the mole said, 'I am glad that none of my children are birds as birds die of cold in the winter.'

As the field mouse and the mole walked ahead, Thumbelina sat down beside the swallow. She put her hand on the bird's breast and felt its heart still beating faintly. 'He isn't dead!' thought Thumbelina happy. 'I won't let you die, pretty bird. Perhaps you had sung to me in the summer.'

New Words | faintly
alarmed

That night, Thumbelina collected ample amount of hay and wove a little matting for the swallow. Later, when the field mouse was fast asleep, Thumbelina tip toed out of the house, stepped into the tunnel and went to the swallow. Gently, she covered the swallow with it.

'Soon, you will be fine,' she said.

New Words | ample
hay

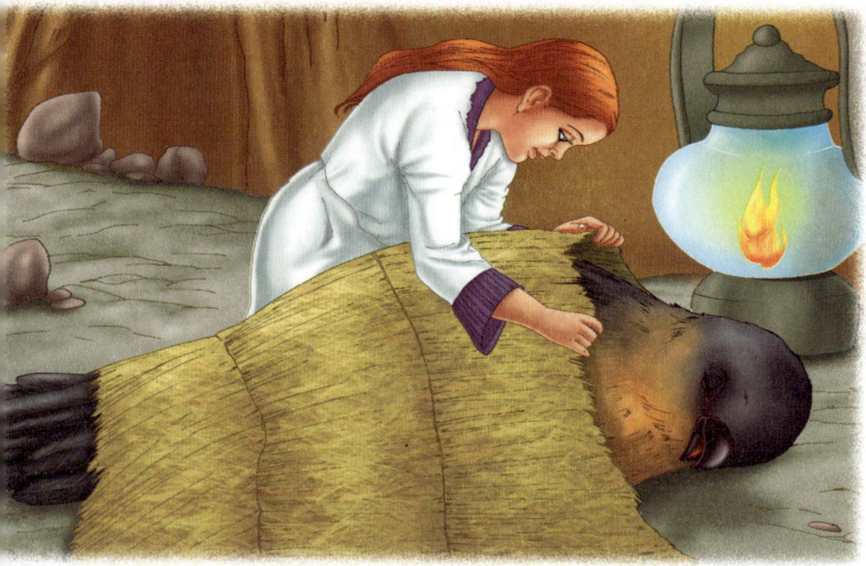

As, she sat there, she felt that the warmth was already reviving the swallow. The next day, while Thumbelina was cleaning the house, the field mouse told Thumbelina, 'The mole wants to marry you. You must get your wedding clothes ready.' The poor girl was stunned hearing this.

Thumbelina protested, 'I don't wish to marry the Mole.'

The mouse said, 'This can't be done. Your marriage has already been settled.'

ew Words	stunned protested reviving

Hearing this, Thumbelina was very sad. She knew that if she married the mole she would never be able to see the sun as the mole lived deep inside the earth. Disheartened, she went to see the swallow for the last time. To her great surprise, she saw that the swallow was flying around in the tunnel. In fact, he had dug a hole in the roof of the tunnel to fly to the surface.

Seeing Thumbelina, the swallow chirped, 'Thank you, Thumbelina. You have saved my life. But why do you look so unhappy?'

'The field mouse wants me to marry the mole who lives deep inside the earth,' said Thumbelina. 'But I do not want to marry him.'

'Come with me, little Thumbelina to the blue skies,' cried the swallow. 'I will take you away from the mole and the field mouse.'

New Words | disheartened

'I will fly with you. I will not marry the Mole,' said Thumbelina happy. She sat on the swallow's back. The swallow then climbed out of the hole and to the surface and with Thumbelina on his back soared high in the air. The swallow and Thumbelina flew over mountains, grasslands and rivers until they reached a beautiful meadow by a huge lake. There, the swallow gently placed

ew Words	soared grasslands meadow

Thumbelina on one of the beautiful flowers that had bloomed in the meadow. Thumbelina was happy now.

Just then, on the flower where she stood, Thumbelina saw a Little Prince sitting in the centre of the flower. She was surprised to see him. He was the king of the flowers!

New Words | bloomed

He was instantly charmed by Thumbelina's beauty and asked her, 'Who are you?'

'I am Thumbelina,' said the little girl.

'Will you be my queen, little Thumbelina? Will you marry me?' said the king of flowers.

Thumbelina agreed. Immediately, many more little men and women stepped out of the flowers. Amidst great cheer and happiness, Thumbelina got married to the king. The swallow sang the sweetest songs on her wedding day. Thumbelina was happy at last.

ew Words | charmed
instantly
cheer

Let's Recall

1. What did the woman wish for?
2. The toad carried away Thumbelina while she slept in her cradle. Why?
3. Who helped Thumbelina escape?
4. Who gave shelter to Thumbelina?
5. Who was the neighbour of the field mouse?
6. Why did Thumbelina agree to go away with the swallow?
7. What happened when Thumbelina was placed on the flower by the swallow?

The Little Mermaid

Let's know about Hans Christian Andersen

The Story *The Little Mermaid* was written by **Hans Christian Andersen** who was a Danish author, fairy tale writer, and poet, noted for his children's stories.

Hans Christian Andersen was born on April 2, 1805, in Odense, Denmark. His father was a poor shoemaker and his mother was a washerwoman. At the age of fourteen, Andersen went to Copenhagen, Denmark, to try his luck.

After trying really hard for a long time, Andersen passed his university exams in 1828. He celebrated the passing of his university exams by writing his first narrative. The story was a success. Andersen quickly released a collection of poems. Andersen began his fairy tale writing by retelling folk tales he had heard as a child. However, soon, he began to compose his own stories. Most of his stories are original. The first volumes written from 1835 to 1837 contained nineteen stories and were called *Fairy Tales Told for Children*.

Deep inside the blue sea, where the sun rays could not reach, stood the kingdom of the Sea King, Triton. His kingdom was more magnificent than any palace built by man. King Triton lived with his old mother and six beautiful daughters.

The mermaids were forbidden to rise above water until they were fifteen. One by one, the princesses turned fifteen. Every time a princess returned from her trips above water, she told a wonderful story. 'I saw beautiful castles,' said

New Words | mermaids, magnificent, forbidden, castles

one. 'I saw huge cities,' said another, increasing the curiosity of the youngest Princess, Ariel.

At last, Ariel too turned fifteen. 'I will now see the land of men!' she exclaimed with joy.

New Words | curiosity

The little mermaid waited impatiently for the evening and then, rose above water. She saw a ship. 'I must take a closer look at this beautiful ship,' said Ariel to her best friend, Flounder, the fish.

New Words | impatiently

As she swam towards the ship, she saw several firecrackers light up the night sky. The night sky was lit with a beautiful display of colours.

The mermaid was wonder struck and said, 'I wonder, what are they celebrating?'

Curious, the young mermaid began swimming near the cabin windows. Then, by a cabin window, she saw a handsome prince, named Eric looking outside towards the sea.

Minutes later, a wild storm arose and as Ariel watched, the ship was caught in the violent waves. Winds howled and lightening struck the ship. Soon, the ship was on fire.

The little mermaid looked on from just beneath the water surface helplessly.

Just then, a huge wave crashed over the deck. In a flash of lightening, Ariel saw that

New Words | display cabin violent howled

Prince Eric was thrown into the sea. As fast as she could in the raging waves, Ariel caught hold of Prince Eric and brought him to the sea surface. The prince was unconscious. Then, in the raging storm, she swam with the prince towards the seashore. The ship along with the sailors had meanwhile gone down into the sea.

New Words | unconscious
raging

When the mermaid had brought the prince to the shore, she remained beside him. Soon, however, he regained consciousness and she had

New Words | regained

to hide herself among the waves. Just then, a young girl saw the prince. She thought that he was hurt and called for help. Then, she took him away in her carriage.

'I wonder if I will ever see him again. The prince would never know that I had saved him,' the mermaid thought sadly. With a heavy heart she swam back to her father's castle.

Everyday, the little mermaid rose above water in the hope of seeing Prince Eric but she never saw him. Luckily, one day she did see him near a beautiful castle. Then, she started visiting that same place everyday.

One day, the mermaid asked her grandmother, 'Grandma, do men live forever?'

'No! They must die but unlike us they have immortal souls that live forever,' said her grandmother.

New Words | immortal

From that moment, the little mermaid was determined to become a human being and have an immortal soul.

'I will ask Ursula, the sea witch for help,' she often thought. One day, Ariel went to the sea witch and told her what she wanted.

'You love the prince and want to become a human. I can help you but in return I want your sweet voice,' said the sea witch.

New Words | determined

The little mermaid agreed for she only wanted to be a human. The sea witch gave her a potion and said, 'Drink this portion at dawn, but remember that you will die if the prince marries someone else.'

lew Words	potion dawn

The little mermaid was very happy and swam quickly towards the prince's castle. At dawn, she came up to the shore and drank the potion the sea witch had given her. At once, she was in terrible pain. It seemed to her that she was burning. When she could bear the pain no longer, she fainted. When she recovered, she saw the prince standing beside her. The little mermaid was filled with joy.

'Who are you?' Prince Eric asked her kindly.

The little mermaid tried to reply but remembered that she would never be able to speak again. The sea witch had taken away her sweet voice. But she did not regret losing her voice. She was near her prince. The kind prince then took her to his castle.

The mermaid now lived in the prince's castle. But as time passed, she realized that the

New Words | recovered
regret

prince only thought of her as his friend. He did not love her. The little mermaid was saddened.

ew Words | saddened

One day, the prince told her, 'Tomorrow, I am going to visit a princess who will be my bride. I want you to come with me.' The little mermaid agreed. Now, the prince's bride turned out to be the same girl who had helped him on the seashore.

Later, as they returned to the prince's kingdom, the little mermaid remembered the words of the sea witch. She thought standing on the ship's deck, 'Though, I have become human, I have not been able to get my love.'

As her thoughts gradually turned to her father and sisters, she thought that her sisters were swimming by the side of the ship. When she looked again, indeed her sisters were looking at her with pleading eyes!

She saw that her sisters' hair was cut short. Surprised, she asked with gestures, 'What are

New Words | deck
pleading
gestures

you all doing here? Why have you all cut your hair?' 'We have given our hair to Ursula, the sea witch, in exchange for this dagger. You must

New Words | exchange

pierce it through the prince's heart. You will once again become a mermaid the moment his blood will fall on his feet. Also, you will not die dear sister,' said her sisters.

The little mermaid took the dagger from her sisters. But as she went towards the prince's room, she stopped.

'I cannot kill the prince,' she thought and flung the dagger into the sea.

The next moment, the sea water turned red. And before his sisters could understand anything, the little mermaid jumped into the sea from the ship's deck.

But instead of falling down into the sea, the little mermaid felt as if she was rising higher and higher into the sky. Hundreds of transparent beings were flying in the air around her.

New Words | pierce
transparent

They surrounded her and said, 'We are the daughters of air. You are one of us now. Come with us. With your good deeds you have earned an immortal soul.' Ariel, the little mermaid got everlasting happiness for she had sacrificed her life for the prince whom she loved.

New Words | deeds
everlasting
sacrificed

Let's Recall

1. Where did King Triton live with his daughters and mother?
2. What did Ariel saw when she swam to the surface of the sea?
3. How did she save the prince?
4. What did the princess want to become?
5. What had she had to give to the sea witch?
6. Whom did she see as she stood on the deck of the ship?
7. What did her sisters give to the sea witch to get the dagger?
8. What did happen when Ariel threw the dagger into the sea?

Sleeping Beauty

Let's know about Charles Perrault

Sleeping Beauty has been written by **Charles Perrault**. He was a French author who lived in the second half of the 16th century. His publication of *Tales of Mother Goose* marked the beginning of a new literary genre, the *fairy tale.* He was one of the first writers in European literature who turned his eyes towards folklore. Perrault was born in 1628 in a clerical bourgeois family. He received legal education and occupied high royal office. Perrault continues to mesmerize his readers till today with his engaging stories and amazing style. Here is a collection of 8 most famous stories of Perrault.

- Puss in Boots
- Cinderella
- Little Red Riding Hood
- Ricky of the Tuft
- Tom Thumb
- Blue Beard
- The Fairies
- Sleeping Beauty

Once upon a time, a king and queen were blessed with a lovely daughter and there was great rejoicing in the kingdom. The king gave a grand feast to celebrate the joyous occasion. The seven fairies of the kingdom were also invited to the feast. However, the king forgot to invite an old fairy.

When the feast had begun, the old fairy came to the palace. She said angrily, 'Doesn't

New Words | rejoicing
joyous

the little princess require my blessings?' The king apologized for his mistake and said, 'I am so glad you had come. Please enjoy the feast.'

Once everyone had eaten, the fairies began giving their blessings to the little princess.

New Words | apologized

However, the youngest princess sensed that the old fairy was up to some mischief. So, she decided to give her blessings in the end. After six fairies had given their blessings, the old fairy stepped forward. She had a wicked look in her eyes as she said, 'When the princess will turn fifteen years of age, she will prick her finger with a spindle and die.' Hearing this, the queen cried out while those assembled were filled with horror. Meanwhile, the old fairy had gone out of the palace. Even the fairies were stunned by what the old fairy had said.

Many suggested that the king should go after the old fairy and plead with her to take back her curse. But the king and queen seemed rooted to the ground. While everyone including the king and queen were filled with grief, the youngest fairy stepped forward. She looked at

New Words	mischief	prick
	curse	grief
	horror	

the princess and said, 'I do not have the power to break the curse of the old fairy. However, I can change it. When the princess will prick her finger on the spindle, she will not die. Instead she will fall into a deep sleep that will last a hundred years. She will wake up with the kiss of a prince after a hundred years.'

The youngest fairy's blessing brought back smiles on the faces of the king and the queen. Soon, the feast ended. At once, the king had it proclaimed that every spindle in his kingdom should be destroyed or kept hidden. The king's command was obeyed throughout the kingdom. In no time, not a single spindle remained in his kingdom.

Years passed by. The princess grew up to be a wise and beautiful young girl. Life seemed safe, for the king had ensured that all the spindles in his kingdom were destroyed. The wicked fairy's curse was almost forgotten. But things were about to change. One day, when the king and queen had gone out for a stroll in the royal garden, little did they know that the old fairy's curse was about to be fulfilled.

New Words	proclaimed	destroyed
	ensured	stroll

That day, the princess was wandering from one part of the palace to the other. It was then that she saw an old tower.

'I wonder what I will find in that old tower,' said the princess and went towards it.

Once there, she began climbing the old, rusty stairs of the tower. Near the top of the tower, she saw a little wooden door. Curious to know what was behind the door, the princess opened it.

Behind the door in a small room sat an old woman spinning using a spindle. The princess had never seen a spindle. She did not even know what spinning was! Curious, she asked the old woman, 'What are you doing, grandma?' 'I'm spinning, child,' replied the old woman. 'Can I spin too?' asked the princess. 'Of course,' said the old woman.

New Words | rusty

But the moment the Princess touched the spindle, her finger got pricked. Immediately, the princess fell into a deep slumber. The old fairy's

New Words | slumber

curse was at last fulfilled. In fact, the old woman was none other than but the old fairy herself.

'Now, no one will dare to insult me,' said the old fairy and vanished in a puff of smoke.

Later, when the princess was found and could not be awakened, the king and queen saw the prick wound on her finger. They understood that the old fairy's curse had been fulfilled.

New Words | vanished
puff

The good fairy meanwhile too had been informed. She then cast a gentle spell over the castle and everyone in the castle immediately fell asleep. Gradually over the years, creepers and thorns grew all over the palace and hid it from view. Only the highest tower of the palace remained visible.

New Words | creepers

As years passed by the story of a beautiful princess sleeping in a palace hidden in the forest spread far and wide. Many princes found the palace and attempted to enter it but the thick undergrowth of creepers around the palace made it impossible for them to even go near the palace.

Then many years later, a handsome prince came to hunt in the forest. He had come visiting that kingdom from a country far away and had not heard about the sleeping princess. While on his hunt, he saw the high towers of the palace from the distance surrounded by thorny bushes.

'What are those towers in the middle of the forest?' thought the prince curious. He asked his attendants about them but no one could tell him anything.

New Words	undergrowth attendants

Filled with curiosity, the prince started towards the towers, leaving his attendants behind.

On his way, the prince met an old man. Thinking that the man may help him, he asked, 'Sir, what are those towers coming out of those creepers?'

'It seems as if you, sir, are not from here. Those towers are the highest towers of a magnificent palace. According to a legend, a beautiful princess has been sleeping there for the last hundred years due to a witch's curse,' said the old man. 'It is said that she will wake up only with a prince's kiss. Many princes have tried over the years to reach the palace but no one has been successful in their attempt.'

Hearing this, the prince said, 'Then, I will too try my luck.'

The prince then thanked the old man and went towards the palace. It so happened that the hundred cursed years had ended just as the

New Words | magnificent
legend

prince made his way to the hidden palace. No sooner had the prince neared the palace that the creepers which hid the way to the palace parted and made way for him to pass.

Filled with wonder, the prince moved towards the palace and soon entered it. On his way, he saw courtiers, soldiers and servants in the corridors fast asleep. At last, he reached the chamber where the princess was fast asleep. Never had the prince seen a maiden so beautiful. He fell in love with the princess immediately. He, next moment, bent down and kissed the princess. Immediately, the curse was broken and the princess woke up from her deep sleep.

The princess was astonished to see the prince. Meanwhile no sooner had the princess woken up that everyone in the palace had woken up too. Everyone was confused to find themselves asleep in the corridors, chairs, in the middle of a task and even on the stairs. The princess had by now recovered herself and realised that the curse had ended.

New Words | courtiers
corridors
recovered

It was then that the prince asked the princess to marry him. The princess bashfully agreed to the proposal.

Just then, the king and queen entered the princess' room. They were so happy to see each other. A few days later, the princess was married to the prince. Of course all the seven fairies were called for the wedding. As for the old fairy, she had died so she wasn't there.

New Words | bashfully

Let's Recall

1. How many fairies were in the kingdom?
2. The wicked fairy cursed the infant princess. What was the curse?
3. What was the blessing of the youngest fairy?
4. How did the princess got her finger pricked?
5. What happened when the princess pricked her finger?
6. What did the prince see in the forest?
7. How was the curse broken?
8. What had happened to the old fairy in the end?

THE HIDDEN HUNTER

Let's know about Folk Tales

The story *The Hidden Hunter* forms a part of the large body of stories called **folk tales**. Folk tales are stories that emerge out of the lives and imaginations of the people of a particular state or country. They are passed on from one person to another or from one generation to another by word of mouth. These tales were not written down, but have existed only in the memory of man. Folk tales often explain something that happens in nature or convey a certain truth about life.

Long time ago, in a village by a lake there lived a great hunter who was invisible. He was called the 'Hidden One'. Everyone knew that any young woman, who would manage to see him, would become his bride.

Many young women kept visiting his cottage at the far end of the village in the hope of seeing him. Each of them was tested by the hunter's sister, who was called the 'Patient One'. But years had passed and none of the young girls

New Words | invisible

of the nearby villages had succeeded in seeing the invisible hunter. But as years rolled by, the efforts to see the hidden hunter did not stop.

In the village where the invisible hunter lived, stayed two sisters with their father. Their mother had died when they were young. The younger sister had a good heart while the elder

New Words | succeeded

one was jealous and cruel. Whenever their father went out for work, the elder sister would torture the younger one by burning her arms and face with glowing sticks from the fireplace. This went on for months altogether.

Each time, the elder sister would threaten her sibling saying, 'Don't you dare tell father or next time it will be worse!'

New Words | torture
threaten
sibling

The poor father kept thinking that her younger daughter was clumsy and kept burning herself. Whenever he told his younger daughter to be careful, she merely bit her lip for she could not tell her father the truth.

Time passed by. The father never came to know about the truth behind his younger daughter's scars. After a while, the younger daughter had so many scars on her body that she was called 'Little Scarface'. She also lost her long braids as her sister burnt them off. She now looked ugly and nobody looked at her.

Whenever, Little Scarface sewed clothes for herself, her elder sister took them from her saying, 'You will not wear any good clothes or proper shoes! I am made for all such good things.' Poor girl could do nothing to stop her sister.

New Words | clumsy
braids

And so, the younger sister had to go wearing rags and remain barefoot as she had no shoes to wear either.

One day, the elder sister put on her finest clothes and elaborately made her hair. When she was thus dressed, she went to Little Scarface and said, 'Do you know where I'm going?'

New Words | elaborately
rags
barefoot

‘No,’ said Little Scarface.

‘I’m going to the cottage of the Hidden Hunter. It is he who I will marry. Of course, that’s something you can never dream of.’

Little Scarface bowed her head sadly and said nothing. After a while, the elder sister went to the house of the Hidden Hunter. Once there, she was greeted by the sister of the hunter.

New Words | greeted

'You are welcome young lady,' said the Patient One. 'My brother will return soon from hunting. Come and help me prepare the evening meal.'

The two women worked for a while in the kitchen. When it was time for sunset, the Patient One led the young woman to the shore of the lake.

'There, my brother comes,' said the Patient One, pointing to the shore. 'Do you see him?'

The young woman could see no one but she decided not to tell the truth. So, she said, 'Of course. There he is!'

The Patient One narrowed her eyes and asked, 'And what is his shoulder strap?'

'A strip of rawhide,' said the young woman, thinking it to be a safe guess.

New Words | narrowed
strap
rawhide

Hearing this, the Patient One frowned. ‘Let us return to the cottage,’ she said simply.

On returning to the house of the Hidden Hunter, the Patient One and the young woman made the remaining meal.

Suddenly, a deep voice said, ‘Hello, dear sister!’

New Words | frowned

The young woman jumped in surprise. She stared at the entrance but saw no one.

'Greetings, brother,' said the Patient One.

As the young woman watched with wide eyes, a shoe appeared on the floor followed by another. Moments later, bits of food rose in the air and vanished into an invisible mouth. The young woman turned to the Patient One.

'When will our wedding take place?' she asked unabashed.

'What wedding are you talking of? Do you think my brother would marry a liar and a fool?' said the Patient One, angrily. The young woman knew her lie was caught and ran back home crying.

The young woman spent the next day in bed, weeping. In the afternoon, Little Scarface came to her.

New Words | entrance
vanished
unabashed

'Sister, let me have some material to make a pair of shoes and new clothes. Now it is my turn to visit the Hidden Hunter.'

'HOW DARE YOU!' screamed her sister. 'DO YOU THINK THAT YOU CAN DO WHAT I COULDN'T? Even if you saw him, do you think he'd marry a horrible looking creature like you?'

New Words	material creature

Saying this, she again started crying. Then, Little Scarface went to her sister and said, 'No matter what you say, I will go to visit the Hidden Hunter.' Her sister was left stunned hearing this.

Without wasting another moment, Little Scarface went to her father's chest and took out an old pair of shoes. Though the shoes were too big for her, she put them on her small feet. Then, she went out of the house and went to meet the Patient One in her cottage.

As Little Scarface walked through the village, the villagers made fun of her.

'Hey, Little Scarface, aren't those shoes too big for you?' called out a young man.

A young woman shouted, 'I think she is going to visit the Hidden Hunter. Little

New Words | stunned
chest

Scarface, did you burn yourself and cut off your hair to look pretty for him?'

Little Scarface ignored all their taunts and laughter and walked on till she reached the cottage of the Hidden Hunter at the end of the village.

When Little Scarface reached the cottage of the Hidden Hunter, she met his sister. The Patient One was surprised to see the young girl but she politely said, 'You are welcome. Come inside and help me with the evening meal.'

New Words | ignored
taunts

Little Scarface, without any hesitation, helped the Patient One in preparing the evening meal. Soon, the evening meal was prepared. As she always did, the Patient One took Little Scarface to the lake at sunset just like she had done with her elder sister.

'There, my brother comes,' the Patient One told Little Scarface happily. 'Do you see him?'

Little Scarface gazed hard along the shore.

'I'm not sure . . . .'

But the next moment Little Scarface's eyes lit up.

'Yes, I see him! How can somebody be so wonderful?' she said amazed.

The Patient One looked at her filled with curiosity.

'What is his shoulder strap?'

'His shoulder strap is . . . the rainbow!'

The Patient One's eyes grew wide.

'And his bowstring?'

'His bowstring is the Milky Way!'

New Words | gazed
curiosity
bowstring

The Patient One smiled this time. 'Let us return to the cottage,' she said.

When they reached the cottage, the Patient One washed Little Scarface with some magical water. The young woman's scars disappeared leaving her skin shining and smooth. Then, she combed the young woman's hair with a magical comb which made her hair grow quickly to her waist. Then she took out a beautiful wedding gown for Little Scarface.

New Words | disappeared

The moment Little Scarface had put on the gown, a deep voice said, ‘Good evening, my dear sister.’

Little Scarface turned and saw the magnificent young hunter. As their eyes met, she saw the surprise in his eyes.

‘Good evening, my brother. You are discovered at last!’ said the Patient One, smiling.

The Hidden Hunter walked over to Little Scarface and took her hands.

‘For years I have waited for a woman of pure heart and brave spirit. Only such a woman could see me. And now, I have found my bride.’

And so they were married. Now, Little Scarface had a new name—the Lovely One.

New Words	pure	spirit
	magnificent	discovered

Let's Recall

1. Who was invisible?
2. What was the name of his sister?
3. How did the elder sister torture her younger sister?
4. Why did the Patient One refuse to let the elder sister marry his brother?
5. What was the invisible hunter's shoulder strap?
6. What was the Hidden Hunter's bowstring made of?
7. Whom did the Hidden Hunter marry? Why?